The Forgotten Puppy

2018

18

Other titles by Holly Webb

The Snow Bear
The Reindeer Girl
The Winter Wolf
Holly Webb's Treasury of Animal Stories

Animal Stories:

Lost in the Snow
Alfie all Alone
Lost in the Storm
Sam the Stolen Puppy
Max the Missing Puppy
Sky the Unwanted Kitten
Timmy in Trouble
Ginger the Stray Kitten
Harry the Homeless Puppy
Buttons the Runaway Puppy
Alone in the Night
Ellie the Homesick Puppy
Jess the Lonely Puppy
Misty the Abandoned Kitten

Oscar's Lonely Christmas
Lucy the Poorly Puppy
Smudge the Stolen Kitten
The Rescued Puppy
The Kitten Nobody Wanted
The Lost Puppy
The Frightened Kitten
The Secret Puppy
The Abandoned Puppy
The Missing Kitten
The Puppy Who Was Left Behind
The Kidnapped Kitten
The Scruffy Puppy
The Brave Kitten

My Naughty Little Puppy:

A Home for Rascal
New Tricks for Rascal
Playtime for Rascal
Rascal's Sleepover Fun

Rascal's Seaside Adventure
Rascal's Festive Fun
Rascal the Star
Rascal and the Wedding

The Forgotten Puppy

Holly Webb

Illustrated by Sophy Williams

For Faith

www.hollywebbanimalstories.com

STRIPES PUBLISHING
An imprint of Little Tiger Press
1 The Coda Centre, 189 Munster Road,
London SW6 6AW

A paperback original
First published in Great Britain in 2015

Text copyright © Holly Webb, 2015
Illustrations copyright © Sophy Williams, 2015
Author photograph copyright © Nigel Bird
My Naughty Little Puppy illustration copyright © Kate Pankhurst

ISBN: 978-1-84715-508-5

The right of Holly Webb and Sophy Williams to be
identified as the author and illustrator of this work
respectively has been asserted by them in accordance
with the Copyright, Designs and Patents Act, 1988.

A CIP catalogue record for this book is available
from the British Library.

Printed and bound in the UK.

10 9 8 7 6 5 4 3 2 1

Chapter One

"It looks weird," Emi said, staring anxiously around the empty room.

"Only because there's nothing in it, silly," her older brother Ben told her. He had a special older-brother voice he used for saying things like that, and Emi glared at him. Just because he was fourteen, it didn't mean he knew everything.

"I know that! It just still looks …
weird. It doesn't look like our house."

"It will when all our things are in it,
Emi, don't worry." Mum was standing
in the doorway holding a box. "In a
week it'll feel like we've always lived
here, I promise. Now, can you two
come and help me unload the car?
The removal van will be here with the
rest of our stuff soon and I want to get
these bits into the kitchen first."

After a last worried look around their new living room, Emi followed them out to the car. There was one good thing about this house, she realized and her eyes brightened a little. Through the window, she could see out into a garden. That had been one of the things that made them all love the place. The garden wasn't huge and it was a bit messy – Mum said all those straggly bushes needed a proper haircut – but at least it was there. The rented flat they'd been living in since Mum and Dad had decided to split up hadn't had a garden at all, just a little concrete yard for the bins.

Emi hurried after Mum and Ben, smiling to herself. She couldn't wait to unpack – getting out her clothes and books would make the bedroom feel like it was properly hers. For the last couple of weeks everything had been in boxes. She wasn't actually sure where anything was, but discovering things again would be part of the fun. She hadn't seen her favourite purple cardigan or her slippers for ages.

And once they were all properly unpacked – settled, Mum called it – then they could start to think about the most important part of the move. It was the most important part for Emi, anyway.

Now they had a garden, Mum had said that at last, after years of *maybe* and *one day* and *when you're older*, they could get a dog.

"Mum…"

"Mm-hm?"

"Mum, are you actually listening? You look like you're thinking about whether that picture's in the wrong place. Again."

It had been five weeks since they'd moved in, and Emi's mum was still worrying about whether everything was in the right spot or not. She blinked and looked at Emi guiltily.

"You're right, I was. Sorry. It just doesn't seem to fit there and it's getting to me. I really am listening now."

"Except for that picture and not liking the shape of the bath taps and the way that cupboard door squeaks in the kitchen –" Emi was counting on her fingers – "do you think we're almost settled in?"

Her mum smiled at her. "I suppose so. Do you feel like we are?"

"Yes!" Emi looked at her pleadingly. "Do you remember – you said that when we were settled, we could think about getting a dog. I don't mean we should actually get one right this minute, but we could at least think about it, couldn't we? What sort of dog we'd like and where we'd get it from? Please?"

Her mum nodded. "I hadn't forgotten, Emi. I've been thinking about it, too. Go and see if Ben's finished that homework he was doing and ask him to come down here for a minute."

Emi raced up the stairs. She was pretty sure that Ben wasn't doing his homework at all – she could hear him talking to one of his mates about the computer game they were playing, but by the time she got upstairs and banged on his door, he had his English essay up on the screen and was looking all innocent.

"What, Emi? I'm working."

It was tempting to point out that he'd only written about three lines, but the last thing Emi wanted was to get into an argument with her big brother. That would be an absolutely perfect way to make Mum forget about getting a dog.

"Mum wants to talk to us. About the dog! Can you come down, pleeease?"

Ben yanked off his headphones and jumped up. He was almost as keen on having a dog as Emi was, especially as he was old enough to remember Alfie, the dog Mum and Dad had owned years ago. Alfie had died when Emi was really little and she couldn't remember him at all.

Emi hurried back down to the living room, with Ben jumping down the stairs after her. When she got there, the little table in front of the sofa was covered in old photograph albums. She glared at her mum. "You said we could talk about dogs!" she cried out. "You're not supposed to be unpacking more stuff!"

Her mum laughed. "I'm not. I was trying to find some photos that I wanted to show you. Look – do you see who that is?"

Emi and Ben stared down at the photo – a little girl with a very serious face and dark hair cut in a fringe. Emi thought the girl looked quite like her, but she didn't remember ever wearing dungarees like that…

"It's you, Mum, isn't it?" Ben said. "Was that in Japan, then?"

"Yes." Mum nodded. "I must have been about six there, I think."

Emi looked at the photo curiously. Mum didn't talk that much about her life in Japan. She'd come to England as a student, and then she'd met Dad, and she hadn't been back all that often. Their Japanese grandparents – Emi and Ben called them *Sobo* and *Sofu*, which meant Gran and Grandpa in Japanese – sent them presents on their birthdays and at Christmas and they called every few weeks, but Emi had only met them once, when they'd come over to visit a couple of years before.

"This is the one I wanted you to see, look." Mum flicked over the page and showed them the same little girl – she even had the same dungarees on – but this time she was sitting next to a dog, with her arm around its neck. Both of them looked so happy that Emi couldn't help going, "Awwww…"

Ben rolled his eyes at her. "You never told us you had a dog when you were little, Mum!"

"So cute… What sort of dog is that?" Emi asked, frowning. She was usually excellent at spotting dog breeds. She had a poster on her wall that had come with one of Dad's newspapers, showing lots of different dogs. But she wasn't sure about this one at all.

"Actually, are you sure that isn't a fox?" Ben asked, peering at the little photo. "It's got a real fox face with those pointy ears! And a bushy tail."

"No, it's fatter than a fox," Emi said thoughtfully. "I know what you mean, though, and it's even foxy-coloured – sort of golden-red."

Mum laughed. "He wasn't a fox. He was a Shiba Inu. They're a Japanese breed. And he was called Kin – that

16

means gold." She smiled down at the picture. "He was lovely. The friendliest dog ever. He used to follow me around when I was little, almost like a babysitter. He'd bark at *Sobo* to tell her if I was crawling too far away and she'd come and pick me up."

"He's beautiful. He looks like he's smiling. What does Shiba Inu mean in Japanese, Mum?" Emi only knew a few words of her mum's language, like her name and Ben's. Her brother was actually called Benjiro, which meant peaceful (Emi thought Mum and Dad had picked pretty badly with that one). But he was always just Ben and most people didn't know he had a Japanese name. With Emi it was the other way round. Her proper name was Emily, but Mum always called her Emi. She'd explained that it meant "beautiful gift". She and Dad had wanted their children to have names that worked in both languages. Emi liked it – it felt special to have two names.

"Inu just means dog," Mum said. "The Shiba bit isn't so clear, though. There's a kind of tree with the same name that goes reddish-gold in the autumn, so that could be it. Or some people think it means small. In one of the old Japanese languages, Shiba means small and they're quite small dogs." She laughed. "Kin only looks big because I was so little…"

"Can you get them in this country?" Emi asked thoughtfully. It would be really cool to have a Japanese dog. And she quite liked the idea of taking a dog like that for walks in the park, where people asked each other what breed their dogs were. She always asked the owners if she didn't know – most people loved talking about their dogs.

"People are just starting to breed them over here." Mum looked at Emi and Ben. "You know I called Mariko at the weekend?" Mariko had been a friend of Mum's since they were students together. She was Japanese, too, and came to stay with them sometimes. "Another friend of hers – Kaii – is breeding Shiba Inus. She was telling me that Kaii doesn't live very far from here. In fact, he's got a litter of puppies right now…"

Ben grinned. "Mum! Do you mean we could have one?"

19

Emi was far too excited to say anything – she just gave Mum the most enormous hug.

Chapter Two

"A Shiba Inu?" Emi's best friend Jess shook her head as they walked through the school playground. "I don't think I've ever heard of them! What do they look like?"

"Really, really gorgeous…" Emi sighed happily. "They're not very big, but they're sort of solid-looking, if you know what I mean? Chunky, I suppose.

Ben said Mum's old dog looked like a fox, because they've got quite pointy faces and hers was an orangey-red colour. But you can get black and tan Shiba Inus, too, and even white ones." She giggled. "Mum showed us some photos online and there was a white Shiba Inu puppy – he looked like a snowball with ears. Their fur's not really fluffy, but it sticks out a bit, he was so roly-poly and cute…"

Jess laughed. "You've fallen in love, Emi!" Then she shivered. "Ooooh, talking of snowballs, I wish the bell would go. I'm frozen. I wouldn't be surprised if it actually snowed soon. I really wanted us to have a white Christmas, but all it did was rain in the school holidays…"

"Maybe we'll get a snow day off school instead – that would be good. Imagine playing with a puppy in the snow…" Emi couldn't think of anything better.

"So, do you know when you're going to get the puppy?" asked Jess. "And can I come over to see it? Please?"

Emi put an arm round her friend's shoulders. "Course you can! But I don't think we'll be getting the puppy for a little while. Mum called the friend of her friend who's the breeder, though, and 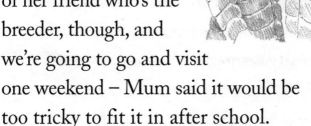 we're going to go and visit one weekend – Mum said it would be too tricky to fit it in after school.

And this weekend we can't, because we're going to Dad's. We're seeing his new flat for the first time. You know he moved, too, right?"

Jess nodded. Her parents didn't live together, either – it was one of the things that she and Emi had in common – that and the fact that they both loved animals. Jess had three cats at her dad's house and guinea pigs at her mum and stepdad's. They both understood what it was like having two families and two houses. Jess knew all about having to remember which house you'd left your homework book in and sometimes forgetting which family was picking you up from school.

"Mum said none of the puppies could come home with us for a few weeks anyway," Emi explained. "They have to be at least eight weeks old before they can leave their mother and they aren't quite that big yet. Nearly though!"

"When you get the puppy, will you be able to take him to your dad's, too?" Jess asked thoughtfully.

Emi shook her head slowly. "I don't think so. It's a pretty tiny flat. Dad's going to have to sleep on the sofa while we're staying, so we'll all fit. And mostly we're going to go by train to get there. Dad can come straight from work to meet us at the station. It's not far from the flat, he says. If he came to get us from our house by car we wouldn't get there till really late. I'm not sure a puppy would like going on a train much."

"You're going by train on your own?" Jess sounded envious.

"With Ben." Emi sighed. "He's going to be a nightmare. Mum and Dad keep saying he's got to look after me, so it's like the ultimate excuse for him to be a bossy big brother. 'I'm in charge, you've got to do as I say, you're only nine, blah blah blah…'"

Jess sniggered and Emi grinned at her. "Well, he *is* like that!"

Emi stood between Mum and Ben on the doorstep of Kaii's house. She was feeling a strange mixture of excited and sad – they were going to meet their new puppy for the first time, so of course she was excited! But she wished Dad was with them. It had been brilliant going to see his new flat last weekend. She'd really missed him when they hadn't seen him for a few weeks because of his move. Dad had played computer games with them, and he'd dragged them out to the woods near his new flat, and even though Ben had said walks were boring, it had been really fun. They'd chased about and jumped over a stream. Emi had nearly fallen in, but Dad had caught her just in time.

There was a little wood near their new house, too, Emi remembered, as she listened to the sound of barking on the other side of the door. They'd be able to take their new puppy on walks there soon! Maybe Dad would get a pet as well, she thought, as Mum smiled down at her. But not a dog – not when he was out at work all day. They were really lucky that Mum mostly worked from home, so they wouldn't be leaving their new puppy alone too much.

"Hello! Erika, yes? And Emi and Ben? I'm Kaii." He beamed at them as he opened the door. His sweater was covered in dog hair but Emi was hardly looking at him because, peering nosily around his legs were two beautiful dogs. The larger dog was black and tan, but the smaller one was the same golden-red colour as Kin, her mum's old dog. Seeing the Shiba Inu breed for real, instead of in a faded photo, Emi realized that they were so much

more beautiful. Their pointed, pricked-
up ears made them look really clever.
They had whitish fur around their dark
eyes, too, which made them stand out.
Both of the dogs were staring at Emi
now, with their heads on one side, as
though they were trying to work out
what they thought of her.

Kaii was laughing, Emi suddenly realized, and so were Mum and Ben. Emi looked up at them, her face going red. What had she done?

"It's OK," Kaii said, smiling. "I was just saying why don't you come in? I don't think you heard a word I said, though. You like them, then?"

"They're *beautiful*!" Emi told him, as they followed him inside. "And they look really clever."

"They are," he agreed. "And they make good pets, too. They're very loving. But you do have to be quite firm with them, otherwise they walk all over you."

"Are these the puppies' mum and dad?" Emi asked. She'd love to have a puppy that grew up like these two.

She was sure they were grinning at her as well. One of them had his tongue hanging out.

"This is Daisuke and this is Kimi," said Kaii. "Dai is the puppies' dad, but Kimi's their big sister. Cho, their mum, is with them in the puppy room at the moment. Would you like some tea first?"

Emi looked at her mum hopefully, and Mum smiled and shook her head. "No, that's OK. Emi's so desperate to see the puppies, I think she might explode if I say yes."

"Come on, then. I've got a room for the mums and puppies at the back of the house – it leads on to the garden, so they can go outside when they're big enough."

It looked like Kaii had had the room built on to the back of his house specially, Emi thought, as he led them through. It must be a lot of work, breeding dogs.

"Here we are. Just come in quietly to start with – Cho's very friendly, but she's quite protective of her puppies. She'll let you play with them in a bit, but we have to let her get used to you."

Emi and Ben practically tiptoed into the room. In one corner another gorgeous golden dog was sitting upright, looking at them sharply. It seemed like she'd heard them coming and had sat up to see what was going on. And next to her, curled up asleep in the big basket, were four fat, furry, puppies, fast asleep.

"Don't worry, they'll wake up in a minute," Kaii told them, as he watched Ben and Emi trying to peer over and get a good look at the pile of puppies. "They have a sixth sense – they always know when something interesting's happening. See? I told you!"

One of the puppies, who was black and tan just like his dad, had popped his head up so quickly that Emi couldn't help laughing. "He looks like a teddy bear," she whispered to Ben and her brother grinned. It was the way the fur stood up all round their heads and paws, Emi decided. As the puppy climbed over his brothers and sisters to come and investigate, he looked like too much of a fluffball to be real.

The other puppies squeaked crossly and woke up as he stomped over them and then Emi gasped. There weren't four puppies – there were five! Now that they were all moving, she could see another puppy who'd been snuggled up next to the mum, with the others on top. And this puppy was a gorgeous golden colour.

"Look…" She nudged her mum.

"I know, they're so cute," Mum whispered back. "Oh, look, they're all waking up now. They're coming to see us!" She reached out and one of the creamy-white pups sniffed her fingers curiously and then licked her.

The golden puppy let out a big yawn and scratched its front paws against the blanket.

"That tail looks like a little doughnut, curled up like that. Is the golden puppy a girl?" Emi asked Kaii. "She looks like a girl…"

"Yes! Well done. She's pretty, isn't she?"

Pretty! Emi wanted to tell him that the puppy was the loveliest dog she'd ever seen, but she didn't want everyone to laugh at her again.

The golden puppy stumbled out of the basket and came to see what her brothers and sisters were looking at. There were new, interesting smells… Exciting smells! She trotted across the room and sniffed at Emi's boots. Then she looked up with dark, sparkling eyes and put her fat little paw on Emi's leg, as if she was saying, *You belong to me…*

Chapter Three

"What will you call her?" Jess asked with a little sigh. "You're so lucky, getting a puppy!"

"We're not sure yet," Emi told her. "We keep arguing about it – it's really difficult to choose. But I like one of the names Mum suggested, Rina. It's pretty just by itself and it means jasmine in Japanese."

Jess nodded. "That's lovely! Oh, look, there's your mum. Email me a picture of her, Emi! Have a good weekend."

Emi waved as she dashed off to meet her mum at the school gate. First they were going to meet Ben (round the corner from his school, though, as he said it was far too embarrassing to be picked up by his mum and his little sister) and then they were driving over to Kaii's house to bring their puppy home. There was a special new metal crate in the back of the car for the puppy to travel in, and at home there was a basket and food bowls and lots of toys.

When they had decided they were definitely going to get the little golden puppy, they'd gone shopping and Emi had darted excitedly round the pet shop, choosing everything the puppy could possibly need and more. Mum had persuaded her to put most of it back, though – the puppy didn't need three leads, after all. Emi knew that really. It was just such fun picking out the different things and imagining the puppy using them and drinking from her new water bowl and playing with all the toys.

Ben had said he thought Emi was so excited she was going to try sleeping in the puppy's basket, but that was just Ben being silly. She had stroked the furry cushion in it, that was all, and tried to think of a little golden puppy sleeping there, all curled up. The basket

was going to be huge for the puppy,
to start off with.

"Come on, Mum, let's go!" Emi
raced down the road, pulling her mum
after her. "Ben had better be quick
getting out of school…"

But Ben was already waiting for
them and he looked impatient, too.

Emi sat in the back of the car, staring dreamily out of the window. She wasn't seeing the streets they drove past at all – she was imagining walks with their puppy and sitting curled up together on the sofa. Or maybe on the floor. Mum wasn't sure about dogs on furniture, but Emi was hoping she'd give in after a while…

The golden puppy heard the doorbell ring and jumped up. She knew by now what that noise meant. Voices at the door and then quite often people coming to see her and her brothers and sisters, and play with them. She liked that – most of the time. Some of the people scared her – they were too loud and picked her up too suddenly. She padded to the door and sniffed at it, hopefully. The day before, one of her brothers had gone away with the people who'd come to visit. She missed him. It had been strange, curling up in the big basket without him last night. She wondered if perhaps this would be the people bringing him back.

But when Kaii carefully opened the door, the golden puppy saw the girl again – the one she remembered from a little time ago. She had snuggled into that girl's lap, she was sure. The girl had rubbed her ears and whispered to her. There had been a boy, too, and he'd thrown a jingly ball for her to play with. He wasn't quite as warm and cuddly as the girl, but she'd liked him, too.

She danced up to Emi and Ben, yapping excitedly and whisking her little curl of a tail.

Emi looked at Kaii hopefully. "Do you think she remembers us?"

Kaii was smiling. "I think so. She hasn't been that friendly to any of the other visitors. She's been a bit quiet today, actually. I think she's missing her brother. He went to a new home yesterday."

"Ohhh…" Emi crouched down to stroke the puppy. "I hadn't thought about that. You're going to miss all your brothers and sisters when you come home with us…"

The puppy leaned into Emi's hand, closing her eyes blissfully. It was definitely the same girl. She knew just how to fuss over a dog. The puppy leaned in a little more and then her claws skittered and scrabbled on the tiled floor and she flipped over.

The puppy stood up, shaking her ears and looking bewildered. She wasn't quite sure what had happened.

But the girl reached down gently and picked her up, holding her close.

"Oh, look at her," Mum laughed. "She's all fluffed up and worried. She's really cute. I do think she looks like a Jasmine."

Ben nodded. "Maybe. But I'm not shouting 'Jasmine' in the middle of the park. Let's go with Rina."

"I can't believe we're bringing you home and we got to choose your name," Emi whispered into Rina's furry ear. "We'll look after you so well, I promise."

Emi was glad they'd gone to get Rina on a Friday night and now they had the whole weekend to get to know her. Kaii had suggested that it would be best to keep her in the kitchen at first, so she wasn't too scared by the big, strange house. But Emi was pretty sure Rina wasn't scared of anything.

Ben put her down on the kitchen floor when they first got home, and she went marching round the room on her little stubby legs, inspecting everything carefully. She stood by the glass back door and barked at a very surprised pigeon, and then they saw her tail wag properly for the first time. Because it was curled up so tightly over her back, she didn't wag it the same way most dogs did. It just wobbled instead.

"Look at her tail!" Emi laughed. "It looks like a caterpillar wriggling!"

"That pigeon got a shock." Ben peered out into the garden. "I think it might be up in the apple tree panicking now."

But Rina looked very pleased with herself. She went back to exploring the kitchen, sniffing at her bed and all her new toys, and looking hopefully at her food bowl. She knew what that was.

"Yes, we'd better feed you," Mum murmured and Rina danced up and down excitedly as she saw Mum opening the bag. After she'd gobbled down the food, she flopped into her new basket. It was too big for her – she looked a bit lost in the middle of it. She sniffed all around it worriedly and then looked up at Emi, Ben and Mum.

"I think she's wondering where the other puppies are," Emi said anxiously.

"Maybe," her mum agreed.

"I've got an idea," Emi said suddenly, rushing out of the kitchen. She shut the door carefully behind her and hurried up the stairs. She was back down a minute later with a huge teddy bear that she'd won in a tombola at the school fair, ages ago. It had dark-gold fur, almost the

same colour as Cho, Rina's mum. Emi
laid the teddy bear down in the basket
next to Rina and the puppy sniffed at
it suspiciously. Then she climbed on to
it, rather slowly, as she was very full of
food, and slumped down, with her head
pillowed on its fat, furry middle.

Emi smiled to herself. The puppy
was already fast asleep.

Chapter Four

"I'm sorry, Rina." Emi sighed and looked down at the puppy, who was nosing at her big rucksack. "You can't come, sweetheart." She put the T-shirts she was carrying into the bag and crouched down to hug the little golden dog. "I really wish you could. I'm going to miss you so much." It was the following weekend, and she and

Ben were going to stay at their dad's. She glanced around the room. "Have I forgotten anything? Oh! Toothbrush!"

She darted into the bathroom and Rina galloped after her. The puppy had only stayed in the kitchen for a couple of days – it was clear that she wasn't at all worried about her new home, even if she did miss the other puppies, especially at night.

The big teddy bear helped, though. Rina had moaned and whimpered for a little while when they had left her in the kitchen that first evening. Emi and Mum and Ben had all sat on the stairs listening to her and worrying. She had sounded so sad that Emi had almost cried. Then Rina had stopped, all at once, and there was no more noise till half past five the next morning. Emi hadn't minded that. She'd gone downstairs in her pyjamas as soon as Rina had woken her up – it just meant an even longer day of playing.

Emi thought they might have to buy Rina a new bear soon, though. She'd chewed most of one arm off already. She pulled him round the house with her too, which was very funny to watch, as the bear was at least twice as big as she was. Emi had filmed her and sent the video to Dad, who said it was the funniest thing he'd ever seen. He was just sorry there was no room for a dog at his flat.

Rina hadn't brought the bear up to Emi's room, as she had enough trouble just getting herself up the stairs.

They were quite steep for a dog with very small legs. She trotted after Emi to the bedroom and peered into the bag again.

She didn't really understand what it was. It looked a bit like Emi's school bag, which was worrying. When Emi had that bag it meant she was going away and she wouldn't be back until just before dinner time. But it never seemed to need this much packing. And Emi was sad, Rina could tell. She kept hugging her, but too tightly, almost so hard Rina tried to wriggle away. Something was different.

"Emi, are you ready?" Mum called up. "We need to go – the train's in twenty minutes."

"Can we take Rina to the station with us?" Emi begged, as she hurried down the stairs to join Ben, with Rina jumping carefully from step to step behind her.

"I suppose so," Mum agreed. "It's not far. I can always carry her back."

Emi reached up to get Rina's lead down from the hook, and Rina twirled and danced and yapped in excitement. Emi's mum had taken her for her last vaccinations on Monday, but she'd only had a couple of very short walks since then.

But why wasn't Emi excited, too? When Emi crouched down to clip on her lead, Rina could tell she was still unhappy. She licked Emi's nose, hoping to cheer her up and Emi giggled, but she didn't sound quite right. She didn't go skipping out into the front garden the way she usually did, either.

Rina stopped, pulling back on her lead as they reached the pavement and whimpering. What was wrong? She didn't want to go out like this.

"Oh!" Emi squatted down next to her. "Do you think Rina can tell we're worried about leaving her behind?"

"Maybe…" Her mum glanced worriedly at her watch. "Perhaps we should take her back inside. You'll miss the train."

"No." Emi stood up and tried hard to smile. "It'll be fine. I want her to see

55

us off. Come on, Rina! Let's go!" And she patted her leg encouragingly.

Rina sniffed cautiously at the fence post and then pattered out on to the pavement. She wasn't sure what was going on, but Emi and Ben were both coaxing her along and there were such interesting outside smells...

Emi stared out of the window of Dad's flat, watching an old lady walking along the street with her dog. The dog was quite elderly, too, Emi thought, and they were walking at a perfect pace for each other, slow and gentle. She heaved a huge sigh, so huge there was a big misty patch on the glass. She missed Rina so much. She couldn't help thinking about her all the time.

She wasn't sure if she wanted Rina to miss her or not. She didn't want the puppy to be sad, but at the same time, it would be nice to know that Rina cared enough to notice if she wasn't there. When they'd got on to the train, she had heard Rina howling on the platform next to Mum. She'd done the same thing the first few mornings when they'd left her to go to school. Mum called it her Shiba scream – she said that Shiba Inus were famous for it – it really did sound as though Rina was screaming.

"Are you OK, Emi?" Dad came and sat on the sofa next to her. "You look a bit down. Too much homework?"

"I've done it all. Sorry, Dad. I'm just missing Rina."

Dad hugged her. "You don't have to be sorry. It's hard to leave her behind when you've only had her a week. You can call your mum later to find out how she is."

But all the same, Emi felt guilty for saying it. She didn't want her dad to think she didn't want to see him – she missed him loads, too. It was just so difficult. She felt like she couldn't ever be in quite the right place…

"Ben, look, there's Mum, I can see her. And Rina, too!" Emi bounced up out of her seat, hurrying to the train doors.

"Leaving your bag on the train, are you?" Ben sighed, picking it up and following her, but Emi was hardly listening. The train was pulling in slowly now and she could see that Mum had picked Rina up to stop her being scared. She was making Rina wave her paw to them.

Emi giggled and pressed the 'Doors Open' button impatiently.

"You have to wait for it to light up, Emi, honestly!" Ben rolled his eyes. The doors beeped and opened.

"Mum! You brought her!" Emi gasped, as she jumped out. "Hello, gorgeous Rina! And you, Mum," she added quickly, kissing her mum on the cheek.

"Did you miss me at all?" Mum asked, but Emi knew she was only teasing.

"How was Rina after we spoke?

Did she mind us being away? Did she notice?"

"She definitely did." Mum put Rina down carefully, now that the train was pulling out, and passed Emi the lead. "She's been really quiet the whole weekend. I'm sure she was waiting for you to come home."

"Oh, poor Rina," Emi murmured.

Ben crouched down to rub the little puppy's ears gently. "We missed you, too," he told her.

"I was glad she was there, though," Mum said, putting an arm round Emi as they walked out of the station. "The house didn't feel so empty. And I might have let her snuggle up with me on the sofa and watch TV last night…" she added, looking a bit guilty.

"You said we weren't allowed!" Emi told her indignantly.

"I know – but we were both missing you two, and she was so cuddly and warm. It's definitely got colder this weekend. I wouldn't be surprised if it snows soon."

Emi looked down at Rina. "You'll love it if it does, Rina. You've got the perfect fur for snow, all thick and soft!"

Rina stood on the back doorstep, watching Emi worriedly. She was dancing about in the white stuff, her boots leaving great deep prints.

It had been cold for ages, but the snow just hadn't come, even though everyone at school had been staring out of the classroom windows and hoping for it for weeks. Another fortnight had gone by, and Ben and Emi had been on another visit to Dad's, and still there hadn't been any snow. But now, at last, it had fallen overnight, just in time for the half-term holiday. Emi had woken Rina up with an excited yell from upstairs and then she'd come racing down in her pyjamas and jumped around the kitchen, practically falling over as she tried to get her wellies on.

Rina sniffed at the snow. It smelled odd – clean and cold and somehow sharp. She wasn't sure she liked it, even though Emi obviously did. Rina let out a huffy little breath. Emi was hers and she had to look after her. She always went outside when Emi did. Cautiously, she put one paw in the snow and then drew it back again at once. Too cold. Too wet.

Emi floundered back across the garden, giggling and shivering. "Don't you like it, Rina? Oh, you have to like it!"

Rina yapped at her crossly, telling her to come in right now. Emi's cheeks were bright red against her black hair and she looked frozen.

"Look!" Emi scooped up a handful of the white stuff and showed it to Rina. It looked like a ball, a white ball. Rina's ears pricked up at once. She loved to play fetch – she and Emi could chase a ball around for ages. Ben had tried to teach her to play football as well, but she wasn't very good at that. The ball was too big and she usually got so excited chasing it that she'd try to fling herself on top of the ball and then she'd fall over.

"Fetch? Fetch the ball!" Emi hurled it across the garden and Rina forgot about the strange white stuff and leaped off the step. She'd bounded halfway across the snow-covered grass before she realized she couldn't actually see the snowball any more.

Emi was doubled over laughing. "Oh, Rina, it's up to your tummy," she giggled.

Rina snorted crossly. But then she decided she didn't mind that much. The white stuff was cold and wet, but the smell was good after all. And she could dig! She scuffled at the snow experimentally with her front paws and it flew everywhere. She sneezed and then she dug and then she chased her tail in the snow and then she dug some more. Yes, she liked this stuff very much…

Chapter Five

It was perfect timing – snow for the holidays. And there was a whole week off school! Emi knew she ought to be happy – and she was, most of the time. Building a snowman and trying to build an igloo (it didn't really work, it just kept collapsing on her head) and going out on Jess's sledge with Rina. It was all brilliant.

But she was spending part of half-term at Dad's and, much as she wanted to see him, she would miss Rina. He'd called her and Ben and told them all about the exciting trips he had planned – there was a science show at the museum, and the shopping centre close to him had set up a mini ice rink. Emi loved the sound of that, she'd never been ice-skating. And he said the woods looked amazing in the snow. There were all sorts of fun things to do. Emi was really looking forward to seeing Dad for a bit longer than a weekend, too. But it did mean four whole days away from Rina.

Emi had missed her so much, the two weekends they had been at Dad's. And she knew that Rina had missed her, too. And Ben, probably, Emi admitted to herself. Rina loved to play rough and tumble roly-poly wrestling games with him, and she quite liked sitting on his lap and watching him play on his computer. Especially when he was talking to his friends. Ben got them to say hello to her, too, and it made her really confused, hearing the voices saying her name coming out of the laptop.

Emi sighed as she stuffed some more clothes into her bag. Rina would be fine. Mum would look after her – and it would be nice for Mum to have Rina, otherwise she'd be lonely while they were away. But still…

"I wish you could come, too," she told Rina, who was sitting next to the rucksack, staring at it suspiciously.

Rina knew what the bag meant by now. Emi was going away. Again!

As soon as Emi turned round to get the rest of her stuff out of the chest of drawers, Rina nudged the bag hard with her nose, so that it tipped over and the clothes spilled out all over the floor.

"Rina!" Emi looked round at her. "Silly! What are you doing?" She crouched down next to the bag and started putting the clothes back inside. But Rina grabbed a pair of jeans in her teeth and pulled them across the room. Then she sat there in the corner with them, looking determined.

"Oh, Rina…" Emi sighed. "Are you trying to stop me from going? I'll miss you, too, I really will. But I have to go and see Dad. Let's go downstairs and get a drink. I'll finish packing later."

Rina followed her out of the room triumphantly, glancing back at the clothes all over the floor. But the bag was still there and the bright curl of her tail sagged a little as she hurried after Emi.

"Are you all packed, Emi?" Mum was smiling, but she looked as though she was trying a bit too hard, Emi thought. She knew Mum missed them when they were away, even though she always said she loved how quiet the house was without Ben, and how she could cook for herself without worrying about Emi saying everything was too spicy.

"I just need to zip up my bag," Emi

said, crossing her fingers behind her back. She was packed, or rather she had been. But she'd have to put back all the things that Rina had knocked on to the floor.

Now where had Rina gone? Emi popped her head round the living-room door, to see if there was a fluffy ball snoozing on the sofa. Mum had given up even saying that Rina wasn't allowed – she was too cosy. But the living room was empty. Emi headed up the stairs. Rina was probably with Ben.

Emi hurried round her room, picking up all the things that Rina had pulled out of her bag. She was a bit worried about how it was all going to fit back in. It still looked really full. But her things had all gone in before…

She knelt beside the bag and pulled it wider open, scooping up a pile of clothes ready to put in. Then she stopped, hugging the jumpers against her as her eyes filled up with tears. That was why the bag was so full. Rina was curled up inside, fast asleep! The puppy had decided that if Emi had to go away again, then this time she was going with her.

Rina stood by the front door, her tail wriggling happily as Emi's mum picked up the lead.

"Not a long walk, though," Mum murmured. "It's still freezing cold out there. And really slippery. The snow melted a bit yesterday and now it's frozen over again. Not so good for walking on, Rina. I haven't got clever claws like you, have I?"

Rina nuzzled against Mum's legs. She wanted to go out so much – they hadn't been on as many walks as usual over the last few days. Mum had a lot of work on, and with Ben and Emi away it was a good chance to get it done. Rina had spent lots of the time curled up on Mum's feet in her little office. They had kept each other warm.

Rina sniffed thoughtfully at a pair of Emi's shoes as she waited for

Mum to get her coat on. Where was Emi? Whenever Emi and Ben had gone away before, they'd come back sooner than this, Rina was sure. It felt as though Emi had been away for a very long time. Rina laid her ears back anxiously, almost forgetting the excitement of the walk. Perhaps Emi wasn't coming back? Perhaps something had happened? What if Emi had forgotten her?

She and Mum had taken Emi and Ben to the station, just like before, so why hadn't they returned? Maybe they were still at the station, waiting? Rina gave a worried little whine. She wanted Emi back now. It must be time to go and fetch her, she was sure. That had to be where they were going now.

Her tail started to wriggle again and her ears pricked forward. She would see Emi soon!

"All right. Let's go." Mum picked up the keys and opened the door. "Just down the road to the park for a bit, mmm? Then back for a nice cup of tea. Maybe some dog treats for you."

They set off, with Rina sniffing hopefully along the snowy pavement, wondering if she would come across Emi's scent, or Ben's. At the end of the road, Mum turned left, making for the park. But Rina stopped, confused. The station was the other way. They were going to the station to meet Emi and Ben, weren't they? She tugged on the lead, digging her claws into the snow.

"It's so icy. Don't pull, sweetheart,"
Mum said. "I don't want to slip over.
Come on."

Rina shook her ears frantically. Mum
was taking them the wrong way. Emi
and Ben would be waiting. She and
Mum might miss them if they didn't
go soon.

She pulled again and let out a
questioning whine, but Mum didn't
turn back towards the station.

"No, Rina," she said firmly. "Come on, we're going to the park. Good girl. That's it."

Rina had been going to puppy classes with Mum and Emi, and the trainer had told them how important the tone of voice was for dog training. *You have to sound as though you mean it*, she'd said. And Kaii had explained to them when they'd first got Rina that Shiba Inus could be hard to train if they didn't know that their owners were their pack leaders. Mum had to be top dog, he'd told them. Mum had practised the firm voice carefully.

So even though Rina didn't want to go down the road to the park, she still did as she was told. She laid her ears back and plodded along like a miserable snail.

But just as they got halfway down the road, Mum slipped over on the ice and let go of Rina's lead. Rina sniffed at her carefully and made sure that she was all right. When Mum started to get up, Rina gave her cheek a quick, apologetic, loving lick. And then she darted away, back down the road, before Mum had a chance to catch her breath and call after her.

Chapter Six

Rina knew the way to the station quite well by now – she had been there several times to drop off and pick up Ben and Emi. So she hurried down the road, her lead trailing over the snow. She could hear Mum behind her, calling her name. She did stop and look back a couple of times. But she knew it was more important to find Emi.

The station seemed different, now that she was here on her own. Had it been this big before, and this busy? There were cars parked all around the entrance, and people talking and hurrying past. Rina tucked herself under a clump of bushes at the edge of the car park and peered out at all the feet as they went past. Now that she was actually here, she remembered the thundering growl of the trains and she wasn't sure she was brave enough to go any further. She had been scared before, even with Emi and Ben and Mum, and now she was all on her own.

But Emi could be so close! What if Rina missed her because she was huddled up and hiding under a bush? Rina waited for the next pair of feet to go thumping past her and then she stuck her nose out, checking to see if anyone else was coming. The car park was quiet. She darted out and followed the man through the gate and past the little ticket office on to the platform.

She couldn't see Emi – but then both times before when Rina and Mum had come to get her, they'd had to wait for a train to pull up and for Emi and Ben to get off. Perhaps she needed to wait for a train now. Rina backed carefully underneath one of the benches on the platform and settled down to wait.

After a few minutes, the bench above her began to vibrate, just a little, and Rina realized that a train was coming. She stood up under the bench and stepped forward a little, watching. There were only a few people on the platform and she could see quite clearly. Her ears pricked up – she would see Emi soon! And Emi would be so happy, Rina was sure.

The noise grew louder and louder, and then the speaker above Rina's head burst into chattering life as well, making her jump. Rina wriggled back under the bench, shivering, and pressed herself against the wall. It was too loud and too frightening! And then the express train blew into the little local station and whooshed past, without even stopping. The people at the edge of the platform just stood there as their coats flapped and the train sped by. Rina watched them, horrified. *How could they stand there, so close to that roaring monster?*

The noise seemed to hang in the air, even after the train had gone and Rina had dared to pull herself away from the wall. How could Emi and Ben have dared to climb on to that great roaring thing? Rina was tempted to go home. She knew the way.

But she had come to get Emi. Emi was on one of those horrible loud things and Rina was going to get her back.

Luckily, the next train was a local one, much slower and quieter as it rumbled into the platform. It was so much less scary than the roaring express that Rina managed to come all the way out from under the bench as it pulled in. She flinched a little at the beeping of the doors, but she was sure she remembered that noise from when Emi and Ben had got off the train before.

But there were so many doors… Rina stood next to a man with a pile of suitcases and watched anxiously as people got off the train. Quite a few of them smiled at her, thinking that she belonged to the suitcase man, or the girl with the headphones standing next to him and not realizing that no one had hold of the little dog's lead.

None of these people were Ben or Emi. Rina whined anxiously. Now the people were all walking away down the platform. The man with the suitcases was picking them up and getting on to the train and so was the girl.

Where was Emi? Rina barked, trying to tell Emi she was here, waiting, but all that happened was

a man in a dark uniform at the end of
the platform turned round and shouted
something. He started to walk towards
her, looking angry, and then the
beeping noise sounded again.

Rina whimpered, feeling frightened.
Emi must still be on the train –
perhaps Emi just hadn't seen her?

Panicking, Rina jumped on to the train, just as the doors began to slide closed. She jumped so fast that she skidded across the floor, sliding into the corner on the other side of the train and landing winded against the opposite doors. She sat there, gasping with fear, as the train pulled away.

After a couple of minutes, Rina sat up straighter. Being in a train didn't feel all that different to the car. And she could move around as she wasn't in her little travel cage. She would go and look for Emi. She had to be here somewhere.

The shouting man had scared her, so Rina didn't want to walk down the gangway between the seats, in case anybody else shouted at her like that.

She would go quietly, she decided, and try not to let anyone see her. She whisked round the little wall by the doors and quickly edged under the first set of seats. The train was mostly empty and she could dart from hiding space to hiding space, occasionally hurrying across the gangway to avoid a set of feet. Every time she stopped she would look hopefully for Emi and Ben, but they were never there.

She was almost at the end of the carriage when she stopped under an empty table. There was a delicious smell of food and Rina was hungry. She sat and looked out at the seats opposite. A mother was sitting there with a baby and a little boy. The boy was eating a sandwich.

It smelled like ham and Rina watched him enviously. She was dribbling, it smelled so good.

The mother was pointing out of the window, showing the baby the view. She wasn't looking at Rina at all. But the little boy seemed to feel Rina's hungry eyes fixed on his food. He leaned over, peering under the table opposite and then he smiled.

Rina gave him a hopeful Shiba smile back – open mouth, tongue hanging out a little. With her dark mouth against the golden fur of her muzzle, it really did look as though she was smiling. The little boy giggled and tore off a piece of his sandwich, holding it out to her.

"Hello!" he whispered.

Rina squirmed closer, crossing the gangway, and gratefully nibbled the sandwich out of his hand. He patted her delightedly, and Rina rubbed her head against his hand. It was so nice to have someone fuss over her.

"Alex, what are you doing?"

Rina scuttled back under the seats behind the table. The little boy's mum sounded cross.

"There was a dog! I gave him some of my sandwich, he was hungry."

"Alex, there isn't a dog, don't be silly. Eat that sandwich yourself, please."

"There is, look! Look, Mummy! He's under the table!"

Rina wriggled back further, as the mother leaned over to look as well.

"Alex, there really isn't! Just eat your lunch!"

The little boy said nothing, but a minute or so later Rina saw a stealthy hand come down past the seat opposite, with the other half of the sandwich and a sausage roll. He dropped them carefully under his seat and then he waved at Rina, obviously trying to show the puppy they were there.

Rina sneaked carefully across the gangway and tucked herself away under the boy's seat, wolfing down the food. Then she gently pushed her cold nose against the boy's ankle to say thank you.

"Dad..."

"Mmmm?"

"Can I ring Mum? Just to check if Rina's OK? She's not used to us being away longer than a weekend."

"Course you can. I was just going to make some bacon rolls for lunch. Then maybe this afternoon we could go and look at the shops down the high street."

Emi nodded. Dad was trying really hard to keep them both happy. It was tricky sometimes, especially with her and Ben liking different things.

"Thanks, Dad." She gave him a hug as she went to pick up the phone. She would ring Mum's mobile, just in case she was out.

The phone rang for ages and Emi grinned, imagining Mum searching through her pockets for it. It was always in the last pocket she checked, or buried at the bottom of her handbag. Mum said she was sure it moved by itself.

"Hello?"

"It's me. Hi, Mum!"

"Oh, Emi! Is everything all right?"

"Yes, it's fine. I just wanted to check

that Rina was OK. Not missing us too much. Are you OK, Mum, you sound a bit stressed?"

There was a breath of silence on the other end of the line and Emi's eyes widened. There was something wrong, she could tell.

"Mum, what is it?"

She heard Mum sigh and saw Dad coming towards her across the living room, looking worried.

"Emi, it's Rina. I fell over on the ice and I let go of her lead. She ran off and now I can't find her. I've been everywhere for the last hour. Home, the park, back again. I've asked all the people I've been past, but no one's seen her. I just don't know where she's gone!"

Chapter Seven

"Alex, come on, it's time to get off."

"But Mummy, the dog… He's still there."

"There isn't a dog, Alex. I checked," the woman said, as she fastened up the baby's snowsuit. "Come on, everyone else is off the train already. If there was a dog, he'll have gone with his owner, won't he? This is the last stop. The dog's going home, too."

Rina saw the little boy lean down, peering under the seats. She almost wriggled further out to see him, but then a man in a dark uniform came hurrying down the train and she stayed hidden. She remembered that other man on the station platform shouting at her.

The little boy followed his mother off the train, still looking round every so often. "Bye, dog!" he whispered, as he stepped off.

Rina poked her nose out from under the seats and looked up and down. No one else was left. The man had gone and the train was empty. Perhaps she should get off, like the little boy? The train had stopped a couple of times before, but then only for a minute or so and more people had got on. This seemed different.

She crept out into the gangway and went to look out of the doors. It was cold out there and starting to get dark. The station looked as empty as the train and it didn't seem familiar at all. For some reason, Rina had thought she would be back where she had started, but this was a completely different place. And where was Emi? This was all wrong! She had come to find her owner and instead she had just got herself lost.

Rina whimpered and peered out at the station, the lights bright and yellowish in the grey of the winter afternoon. Perhaps she had better get out and look for Emi. After all,

Emi definitely wasn't in this train, so there was no point staying here.

Just as she made the decision and stepped forward, the doors beeped suddenly and then slid shut with a thump.

She was trapped.

"Emi, don't panic. It'll be all right, we'll find her," said Dad.

"But Mum said she's asked everyone! She says she doesn't know where Rina's gone!" Emi gasped. She turned to her brother, who looked equally worried.

"Well, we'll go and help her look, then," said Dad. "Come on. You were going back tomorrow morning anyway and you're not going to have a good time here this afternoon when you're worrying about Rina. I'll come with you and we'll all search for her. We'll get the train back, it's a lot quicker than going in the car. Pass me the phone, Emi. I'll call your mum and explain. Go and pack up your stuff. And don't forget to look in the bathroom!" Dad called after her, but Emi had already disappeared to find all her things.

It was the fastest packing she and Ben had ever managed, and they were ready to go only ten minutes later. Dad had checked the timetable and he said there was a train very soon, but he wasn't quite sure they'd make it, with the walk to the station, too. Emi was determined that they would, though. She didn't care that there was another train not long after. She wanted to get back home at once.

Rina sat by the train doors, whining. What was she to do now? The lights had gone off when the doors slid shut and she was all alone in the dark train. She could still see, of course, but the train felt odd in the dark – too quiet. She didn't understand what was happening. Emi was supposed to have been on the train and now she had lost everybody, even Mum.

Rina lay down next to the doors, resting her nose on her paws and whimpering miserably. What if she was stuck here?

Then a sudden beeping noise made her sit up. The doors! The doors made a noise like that! Rina looked up, but the doors didn't move. The noise was from further down the train.

She got up and went to look. A lady

had opened a set of doors at the other end of the carriage and climbed on, with a big black bag. The lights came on again and Rina watched as the lady closed the doors and then moved down the train, humming to herself and picking up all the rubbish that had been left behind.

Rina didn't care if the lady saw her or was cross. She just wanted to get off the train now. The puppy padded down the gangway towards the lady and then stood next to her and barked.

The cleaner had earphones in and she was humming along to her music. She only half heard the bark and then she looked down and noticed a dog right next to her – a dog that had appeared out of nowhere.

The cleaner was so shocked that she dropped the rubbish bag. She didn't like dogs all that much, especially when they crept up on her. She darted down the carriage and unlocked the doors, hurrying off the train to catch her breath and tell one of the platform staff that there was a fierce dog on the train and it had tried to bite her.

Rina stared after the lady in surprise. She had no idea why she had run away. But she had left the doors open and that was what mattered. Rina raced forward and jumped off the train at once, before they could shut on her again.

She stood on the empty platform, looking around uncertainly. Where should she go? Could Emi be here somewhere? Wearily, she walked along the platform, avoiding the patches of snow, and started to climb the steps at the end. She didn't really know where she was going. But Emi definitely wasn't on that train, so she would just have to keep looking.

She padded along the tunnel-like footbridge to the other platform and then looked worriedly at the steps on the other side. They were quite steep, not like the stairs at home. She was used to those now and she could run up and down them without thinking. These steps were metal and open at the back, and they looked slippery.

Rina picked her way down them carefully, wishing her lead wasn't dangling down. It kept getting tangled in her paws.

At the bottom of the steps was
a ticket office and a waiting room,
which looked warm and bright.
But its glass door was tightly closed
against the cold and Rina couldn't see
how to get in. She sniffed at the door
sadly and then trailed past, looking
out at the busy road that ran in front
of the station.

A tall man came hurrying in,
glancing up at the clock outside the
ticket office. He didn't see Rina, but
he tripped over her lead. He yelled as
he almost fell over in the greyish snow
that had been brushed to the side of
the walkway.

Rina didn't stay to be shouted at
again. First the man in uniform at the
other station, then the lady with the

rubbish bags and now this. Mum and Emi and Ben didn't shout at her – or only the time that she'd chewed Ben's trainers, and then Emi had given her a hug, even though Ben was cross. She scurried round the corner of the building and hid behind a ticket machine. There was a little gap there, just wide enough for a very small dog. She would stay there and wait for Emi, out of the cold wind.

Rina wriggled herself comfortable – as comfortable as she could – and peered out, watching the people arrive for the next train. But the thud of feet and the muttering of the announcements blurred together and she rested her nose on her paws and fell asleep.

Chapter Eight

"Dad, run!"

"Emi, honestly, we won't get to it in time. I've got to buy my ticket, remember. Don't worry. There's another train not long after." He pulled out his wallet and started to tap the screen on the ticket machine.

"It's still there…" Emi pleaded, looking up at the departures board.

"Couldn't we try? It's so cold now and it's starting to snow again. I hate thinking of Rina outside in this weather, all on her own. Oh, it's nearly going! Couldn't we go and wait by it and just say that you're coming in a minute?" She gazed across to the other platform, watching the train.

Ben gave her a hug. "It's only fifteen minutes till the next one, Emi. We'll get home and find her. It'll be all right."

"But what if we don't?" Emi said miserably. "What if we've lost Rina forever?"

Ben shook his head. "I bet she hasn't gone far. I know Mum's looked for her, but Rina's probably scared being out on her own, that's all. She's not used to it. She's hiding somewhere really close to home and she'll come out when she's feeling a bit less frightened and we'll find her."

Dad pulled his ticket out of the machine.

"Is it still there? Come on, then, let's run!" cried Emi. "We've got to find Rina!"

Rina twitched in her dream, thinking that she could hear Emi calling her name. Then she sprang up, shaking her head.

She *had* heard Emi! Emi was close by!

Rina stuck her nose out from behind the ticket machine, looking around desperately. She was still a little dazed from her cold sleep, but she could see the train on the other side of the station. Could Emi be on it?

Rina darted out, yapping, calling to Emi to stop, to wait for her. But as she tried to run, something dragged at her, pulling her back.

Her lead was caught! Rina whined

out loud – Emi was just over there, she was sure of it. She had found Emi at last and now she couldn't reach her!

"Goodness me, what's the matter? Are you lost?" An old lady was standing in front of her, looking down at her worriedly. "Poor little thing."

Rina ignored the lady, pulling again at her lead. She had to catch Emi!

"Oh, you're stuck. Stand still, silly thing. There." She reached over and unhooked the lead from the piece of broken brick it was caught up on. "Now, who do you belong to? Oh!"

Rina was gone, not even stopping to let the old lady stroke her. She was scrambling up those slippery metal steps and racing across the footbridge.

But when she got to the top of the steps, the train was gone. She could just see it, in the distance. She had lost Emi again! Rina sat down at the top of the steps and howled and howled.

"We were so close!" Emi sat down on the bench in the little waiting room and put her hands over her eyes. She knew it was stupid to cry about missing a train, but every minute mattered. What if Rina was hiding somewhere, just waiting for Emi to come and find her?

Ben made a face. "I know – I think they could have held on, honestly. Thirty seconds earlier and we'd have caught it. What is *that*?"

A high-pitched yowling was echoing across the station and all three of them peered out of the waiting-room windows, trying to see where it was coming from.

"It sounds like a cross between a police car and a baby," Dad said, smiling a little. "That is one miserable dog. Oh, Emi, don't be sad, I'm sure there's nothing wrong with him – it's probably waiting in a car outside the station, that's all."

"It sounds like Rina when we leave her behind!" Emi whispered, getting to her feet. "But it can't be…"

"It does sound like her," Ben said, nodding.

"Really?" Dad frowned. "It seems unlikely… She couldn't have followed you on to a train, could she?"

Emi and Ben exchanged doubtful glances. "Well, she has been to the station a few times to see us off. But she wouldn't get on a train…"

"I bet she would," Ben said. "If she thought you were on it, Emi. You know she misses you loads."

"It *is* Rina…" Emi said, running to the door as a particularly loud wail echoed across the station. "It sounds just like her. It is!"

She darted out on to the platform, looking around wildly. And there, up at the top of the stairs, was a little dog, with her head lifted up, howling in misery.

"Rina!" Emi screamed, and Rina stopped mid-howl and stared.

Emi hadn't gone after all. Emi was right there! Barking joyfully, Rina hurled herself down the stairs and into Emi's arms.

"You know, if we hadn't missed that train, we might never have found her," Emi said thoughtfully, looking at Rina sitting next to her on the platform. "I think about it every time I go on a train now."

It was several months later and Emi and Ben were with their dad at the station. But this time it wasn't because they were going home – they were going on holiday!

Dad smiled at her. "Aren't you glad I was so slow getting my ticket that day? Have you got your ticket, by the way, Emi? And all your bags? I really don't want to miss this train."

Emi looked down at the bags by her

feet and counted
them hurriedly.
"No, it's all
right, I've got
everything.
I thought for a
minute I hadn't got
Rina's bag, with her bed and her bowls
and all her toys, but I have."

"That dog's got more luggage than
you and Ben," Dad said, grinning.

"Thanks for letting her come on
holiday with us, Dad." Emi put an
arm round his waist. "It's going to
be brilliant, taking her to the beach.
Oooh, the train's coming!"

Rina stood up, looking at the train
suspiciously. It was the first time she
had been on one of these great loud

things since Emi and Ben and Dad had brought her home. She still didn't like trains very much. She hated going to the station to say goodbye to Emi. Though at least now she knew that Emi would always come back.

But this time it was different. Emi was holding her lead and her bed was in a bag – Rina could smell it – just next to them. Rina was almost sure that she was getting on this train, too.

"Are you ready, Rina?" Emi whispered. "We're going on a trip."

Rina squashed herself tightly up against Emi's leg as the train drew in and everyone picked up their bags.

She was not going to let Emi get lost again...

Look out for Holly Webb's 30th
Animal Story, publishing April 2015

The
Secret
Kitten

From best-selling author
HOLLY WEBB

Stripes have lots of exciting plans
to celebrate so keep an eye on
www.hollywebbanimalstories.com
for full details nearer the time!

HOLLY WEBB

Holly Webb started out as a children's book editor, and wrote her first series for the publisher she worked for. She has been writing ever since, with over ninety books to her name. Holly lives in Berkshire, with her husband and three young sons. Holly's pet cats are always nosying around when she is trying to type on her laptop.

For more information
about Holly Webb visit:

www.holly-webb.com